1SE9560Q
D09563S1

Pokémon
SUN & MOON
1
STORY
Hidenori Kusaka
ART
Satoshi Yamamoto

Professor Kukui

A Pokémon researcher with a laboratory on Melemele Island. An expert on Pokémon moves who likes to experience them used against himself!

Sun

One of the main characters of this tale. A young Pokémon Trainer who makes a living doing all sorts of odd jobs, including working as a delivery boy. His dream is to save up a million dollars!

Moon

One of the main characters of this tale. A pharmacist who has traveled to Alola from a faraway region. She is a self-confident, original thinker. She is also an excellent archer.

Dollar (Litten)

Cent (Alolan Meowth)

Introduction

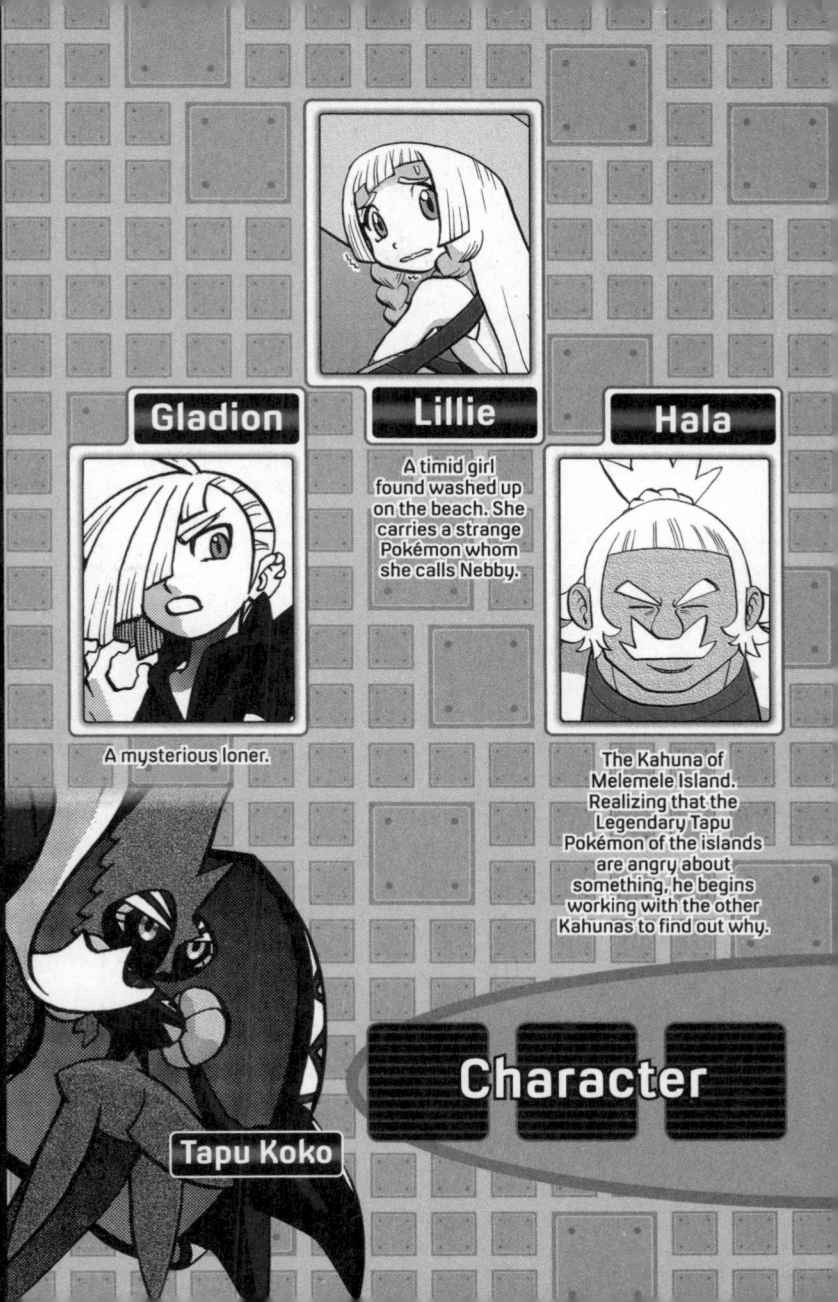
Lillie
A timid girl found washed up on the beach. She carries a strange Pokémon whom she calls Nebby.
Gladion
A mysterious loner.
Hala
The Kahuna of Melemele Island. Realizing that the Legendary Tapu Pokémon of the islands are angry about something, he begins working with the other Kahunas to find out why.
Character
Tapu Koko

CONTENTS

ADVENTURE 1 The Grand Entrance and Delivery Boy Sun 07

ADVENTURE 2 The Delivery of Rotom and the Girl 23

ADVENTURE 3 Pokémon Move Specialist Professor Kukui 49

Zzt zzt...♫

MY GREAT-GRANDSON IS ON THE VIDEO-PHONE!
COME ON! LOOK IN THIS DIRECTION! PLEASE...?

I'M NOT OFFEND-ED, GRAND-PA!
THAT'S OKAY!
SOR-RY...
THEY'RE SNOBBY POKÉMON.
...SUN.

APPARENTLY THEIR PAMPERED HISTORY HAS MADE THEM RATHER... CONCEITED.
WELL, OVER HERE, THEY USED TO BE GIVEN TO KINGS AND QUEENS AS GIFTS.

OH, RIGHT. I GUESS THEY LOOK VERY DIFFERENT FROM THE MEOWTH WHERE YOU LIVE.
RARE ...?
IT'S JUST SO COOL TO SEE SUCH RARE POKÉMON!
YEP! THE MEOWTH IN YOUR REGION ARE SO MUCH FANCIER!

WELL, I HOPE I GET TO VISIT YOU SOME-DAY!
I SEE...

Adventure 1
The Grand Entrance and Delivery Boy Sun

...TROPICAL CLOTHES...
ALSO...
SPLORCH

EWWW! WHAT IS THIS GOOP ?
YOU OKAY?
AHHH! MY BAD! MY BAD!
...WELL... THEY'RE KIND OF SLIMY. AND ONE SLIPPED OUT OF MY HAND, AND... SORRY.
I WAS TOSSING PYUKUMUKU BACK INTO THE SEA FOR MY PART-TIME JOB, BUT...
...BUT NOW MY CLOTHES ARE ALL GOOPY. SO YOU NEED TO REIMBURSE ME FOR A NEW OUTFIT.
I'VE GOT AN IMPOR-TANT DELIVERY TO MAKE...
YOU OWE ME...
WHAT'S THAT NOW?
IS THERE A PROB-LEM ?!
UM...
YOU MEAN WITH... MONEY ?!
R-REIM-BURSE ?!

...NOT !
ibadoink
YOU'RE RIGHT! MY SKIN FEELS SO SILKY SMOOTH NOW! I CAN'T THANK YOU ENOUGH...
ALL THE CELEBRITIES ARE USING IT. SO, ACTUALLY, YOU OUGHT TO BE GRATE—
...THAT PYUKUMUKU GOOP IS AN EXCELLENT MOISTURIZER!
BUT ...

WHAT KIND OF A PART-TIME JOB IS THAT ANYWAY?!
SPLASH
NO, NO! YOU'RE SUPPOSED TO THROW THE PYUKUMUKU BACK INTO THE SEA! AS FAR AS YOU CAN, TOO!

SEE ...?
rstl
rstl

200 Pyukumuku
JPN ENG FRA GER ITA KOR SPA CHS CHT
Sea Cucumber Pokémon
Water
Height: 1'00" Weight: 2.6 lbs.
These Pokémon line the beaches. The sticky mucus that covers their bodies can be used to soothe sunburned skin. How convenient!
Appearance/Cry
Habitat

PYUKUMUKU, THE SEA CUCUMBER POKÉMON...
I THINK THEY'RE CUTE, BUT THE TOURISTS FREAK OUT WHEN THEY SEE A LOT OF THEM LYING ALL OVER THE BEACH.

SO THROWING THEM BACK INTO THE SEA IS FOR THEIR OWN GOOD.
...WHETHER OR NOT THEY HAVE A STEADY FOOD SUPPLY.
AND WHEN PYUKUMUKU FIND A LOCATION THEY LIKE, THEY HAVE A BAD HABIT OF STICKING AROUND...

WHY...?
IT'S THANKS TO MY BROKEN LEG THAT I'M ONLY WORKING PART-TIME NOW. OTHERWISE I'D BE WORKING NONSTOP!

WHY ARE YOU WORKING WITH A BROKEN LEG?
UM... WHAT'S WITH THE CAST?

YEAH. SO I CAN'T GIVE YOU CASH FOR NEW CLOTHES RIGHT NOW. BUT I PROMISE I'LL MAKE IT UP TO YOU. I'M ALMOST DONE WITH THIS JOB, SO IF YOU JUST HOLD ON FOR A MINUTE...
A MILLION... DOLLARS ?!
SPLASH

TOSS
TOSS

I HAVE TO MAKE A MILLION DOLLARS AS FAST AS I CAN!

ARE YA DONE? OR NOT?
THE DEADLINE IS *NOW*, ODD-JOB BOY.

YEEAAH! THE BEACH IS COMPLETELY PYUKUMUKU FREE!

OKAY, TIME'S UP!

I'M DONE, I'M DONE! GO AHEAD AND CHECK!

IF YOU AIN'T DONE, WE AIN'T GONNA PAY YA.
YER S'POSED TO HAVE ALL THE PYUKUMUKU OFFA THIS BEACH BY THREE O'CLOCK.

GO ON!
SCURRY
SCURRY

HUR-RAY!
ALL RIGHT, HERE'S YER DOUGH.

IT'S TRUE. THEY'RE ALL GONE.
HMM.

drop

HUH ?
tug

NO CLEAR BEACH, NO PAY.
HEY!
THERE'S ONE LEFT.

THE FESTIVAL STARTS TOMORROW, AND THAT'S OUR CHANCE TO MAKE THE BIG BUCKS. IF WE DON'T GET ANY CUSTOMERS ON THIS BEACH, IT'S GONNA BE A HUGE LOSS FER US.
THIS BEACH IS TEAM SKULL TERRITORY.
DON'T-CHA GET IT, BRAT ?
NO WAY!

WE'RE WILLIN' TA NEGOTI-ATE.
BUT... WE AIN'T MONSTERS.

I SAW THE GIRL BEHIND HIM PULL A PYUKUMUKU OUT OF HER POCKET AND–
JUST TELL THEM NO!

...AND WE'LL PAY YA HALF OF WHAT WE WERE GONNA PAY YOU FOR THIS PART-TIME GIG. NAH...HOW ABOUT TEN PER-CENT...?
YEAH. YOU CAN KEEP ON TOSSIN' PYUKUMUKU INTO THE SEA FER THE REST OF YER LIFE...
REALLY ?! YOU ARE ?!

HUH? SHE YOUR GIRL-FRIEND, ODD-JOB BOY?
LOOK! SHE'S STILL GOT SLIME ON HER HANDS!
DON'T! SSHH!
WHIP!
SIGH...
HAVE A NICE LIFE.
YER GONNA HAFTA PAY FOR ITS MEDICAL EXPENSES.
AWWW... YOU'VE BROKEN ITS TAIL!
WHOA! YOU OKAY, SALANDIT?
flk
flk

kra
kakk
SWFFF

IT SHOULD HAVE HEALED BY NOW...
tnk
tnk
whoa

BOOM

IT'S BLOCKING ALL OF THEIR MOVES SIMULTANEOUSLY?!
wff
wff
wff
wff
wfff
WHAT? YOU WANT A PIECE OF ME ?!
ALL RIGHT! TIME TO FINISH THIS...
PAY DAY!
KACH
ING

YOU'RE GONNA BE SORRY FOR THIS!
GYUR-RRGH!

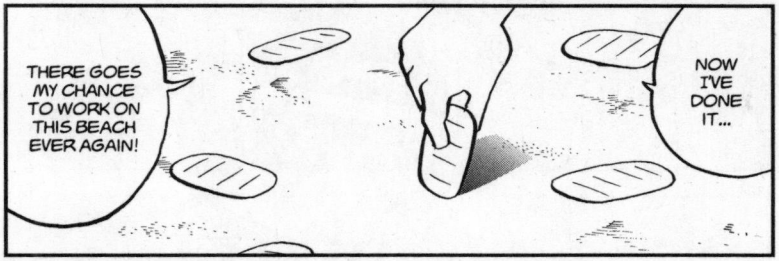
THERE GOES MY CHANCE TO WORK ON THIS BEACH EVER AGAIN!
NOW I'VE DONE IT...

THAT'S A SE-CRET.
FOR A MILLION DOLLARS? WHAT DO YOU NEED ALL THAT MONEY FOR ANYWAY?

I CAN THINK OF A FEW REA-SONS... A MILL-ION OR SO...
WHY WOULD YOU STOOP TO WORKING FOR JERKS LIKE THEM?!

MY REAL BUSINESS IS DELIVERING PACKAGES!
NO PROB-LEM!

HOW ABOUT IF I DELIVER YOUR PACKAGE FOR YOU?
YOU SAID YOU HAD AN IMPORTANT DELIVERY TO MAKE.
ANYHOW, ABOUT ME MAKING IT UP TO YOU...
WHAT? ARE YOU SURE? THAT WOULD BE GREAT, BUT—

TING
LET'S SEE... THERE'LL PROBABLY BE A LOT OF BOULDERS ALONG THE WAY, SO I'LL GO WITH TAUROS CHARGE.
Charge
Gallop
Paddle
NO PROBLEM! I'LL USE MY RIDE POKÉMON.
PROFESSOR KUKUI'S POKÉMON RESEARCH LABORATORY.
WHERE DO YOU WANT IT DELIVERED...?
ABOUT YOUR WET CLOTHES...
I CAN USE THIS TO DRY THEM!
BOM
DOLLAR!

...IT'S ONE MORE TO-WARDS ...
...MY MILLION!
WELL ...
WHY'D YOU NAME YOUR POKÉMON DOLLAR?
FOO
FOO
FWOOSH
EEK!
HOT! HOT!
I'M IN THE BLACK!
Cha-ching
Cha-ching
...GOOD!
MINUS NECES-SARY EXPENSES, THAT'S...
SIGH... THE PYUKUMUKU PART-TIME JOB WAS A LOSS... BUT AT LEAST I EARNED SOME MONEY WITH PAY DAY.
BUT YOU CAN CALL ME...
...SUN THE DELIV-ERY BOY!
MY NAME IS SUN.

A Cheerful Greeting
Here in the Alola region, people greet each other with the word "Alola."
It can mean hello, goodbye and so on, and can be used in a variety of situations. It's even more expressive when you say it while moving both hands in front of your chest in a circle.
Guide to Alola 1

Adventure 2
The Delivery of Rotom and the Girl

Check out the secrets of Sun's delivery service!

SO YOU LET A KID BEAT YOU DOWN...
...AND THEN YOU COME RUNNING TO ME?

IS ANYONE ALLOWED TO MESS WITH TEAM SKULL?!
NO, RIGHT ?!

WE'RE SORRY, MASTER GUZMA!
UM... ARE WE GONNA GET PUNISHED FOR THIS?

PYUKU-MUKU, I BLAME YOU!
FWAP

THEN I, THE LEADER OF TEAM SKULL, WILL PERSONALLY TEACH HIM A LESSON!
REPORT BACK TO ME THE MOMENT YOU CATCH A GLIMPSE OF THAT ODD-JOBS KID AGAIN!
I NEED YOU TO PREPARE THE GRILL STALL.
THE FESTIVAL IS TOMORROW.

BUT YOU CAN CALL ME...
...SUN THE DELIVERY BOY!
MY NAME IS SUN.

trot trot trot trot

trot trot trot trot

Sigh...
SO... WHAT EXACTLY AM I SUPPOSED TO DELIVER TO PROFESSOR KUKUI'S POKÉMON RESEARCH LAB...?
I TOTALLY FORGOT TO GET THE PACKAGE FROM YOU!
MY BAD! MY BAD!
trot
OH, OKAY! UM... HERE'S A DELIVERY SLIP FOR YOU.
SKRIBI
...AND ME!
YOU'RE SUPPOSED TO DELIVER THIS ROTOM...
Delivery Slip
RECIPIENT'S ADDRESS
HAU'OLI CITY OUTSKIRTS
NAME
PROFESSOR KUKUI
RESEARCH LABORATORY
SENDER'S ADDRESS
BEACH
Time of Delivery
EARLY EVENING TODAY
8:00–10:00
10:00–12:00
12:00–14:00
14:00–16:00
16:00–18:00
18:00–20:00
ITEMS
GIRL, ROTOM
Breakable
Perishable
Fragile
Hazardous
GIRL
NOW IT'S OFFICIAL! I'VE ACCEPTED YOUR PACKAGE FOR DELIVERY!
02
LET'S GO!
STK
AND THE LABEL GOES ON THE PACKAGE TOO!

WE'LL GET TO THE HAU'OLI CITY SHOPPING DISTRICT SOON.
IT'S ONLY A SHORT RIDE FROM THERE TO THE LAB.
IS THIS YOUR FIRST TIME IN ALOLA?
YES.
I ONLY CAME HERE TO DELIVER ROTOM.

HEY THERE, SUN!
OOH, ARE YOU ON A DATE?

ALO-LA!
SHEF
A-ALO-LA...

NO, NO! THIS IS WORK!
SHE'S MY PACK-AGE— I MEAN, MY CUS-TOMER!
THIS IS HER FIRST TIME IN THE ALOLA REGION!
SAY HELLO!

SMOOCH
I DON'T NORMALLY DO STUFF LIKE THIS...
HA HA HA HA! GOTCHA! GOTCHA!
EEK! WHAT THE–?!
grrrrr
I SAID I WAS IN A HURRY, DIDN'T I?
C-COME ON...
YOU THOUGHT IT WAS A LEI, DIDN'T YOU?! BUT IT'S THE POKÉMON COMFEY!
roll
THEY PLAYED THAT PRANK ON ME WHEN I FIRST CAME TO ALOLA TOO!
OF COURSE I AM! PROFESSOR KUKUI AND I ARE BUDDIES, YOU KNOW!
ARE YOU GOING TO GET US THERE OR NOT?!

IT WAS PROFESSOR KUKUI WHO GAVE ME...
...DOLLAR AND THIS POKÉDEX!

AND DOLLAR IS A POKÉMON CALLED LITTEN AND...

SO THAT'S A POKÉDEX, HUH...?
YEAH!

HEY, DO YOU HAVE TIME TO BE CHATTERING ON LIKE THIS?
YOU'RE IN A HURRY, AREN'T YOU?
But you're the one...!
OW...!
PANG

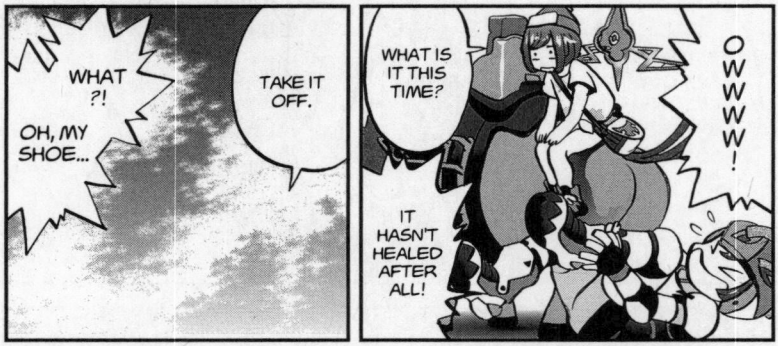
TAKE IT OFF.
WHAT ?!
OH, MY SHOE...
OWWWW!
WHAT IS IT THIS TIME?
IT HASN'T HEALED AFTER ALL!

klt
tr

I CAN APPLY SOME PAIN-KILLER HERE. THAT OUGHT TO DO THE TRICK.
HMM...

NEPU LEAVES... I SHOULD HAVE ENOUGH.
HONEY... CHECK.
MIRACLE SEED... CHECK.
POW-DERED CUBONE SKULL... CHECK.

CLOSE, BUT NOT QUITE.
YOU CAN MAKE MEDICINE? ARE YOU A DOCTOR? A NURSE?

I HAVEN'T INTRODUCED MYSELF YET, HAVE I?
MY NAME IS MOON.
I'M A PHARMACIST.
BEACH
GIRL ROTOM
GIRL

OH, PIKIPEK!
THOSE FLYING-TYPE POKÉMON ARE EATING THEM! TALK ABOUT BAD TIMING!

OH...!
NOW ALL I NEED IS A SPICY BERRY...

I'M GOING TO HAVE TO POLITELY ASK THE PIKIPEK TO STOP FORAGING FOR A MOMENT.
rsti
rsti
OH WELL...

Sigh

HEY! THEY WON'T STOP!

SHAK
A BOW AND ARROW ?!
WHAT ARE YOU ...?!
SHUSH! LET ME CONCEN-TRATE!
uuu
uunk
twang

FFFFFPP
FFFF
I MAKE THE PIKIPEK MOVE AWAY WITH THE FIRST ARROW ...
...AND THEN...
TWANG
TANK

BOM
COOL! CENT, GO FETCH IT!
fwmp
WOW!
shff
shfff
shff
I NAMED IT CENT 'CAUSE IT'S SO LAZY IT'S PRACTICALLY WORTH-LESS.
HA HA HA! IT'S ALWAYS LIKE THIS WHEN IT'S NOT IN A POKÉMON BATTLE.
WAIT... IS THIS THE SAME MEOWTH THAT WAS FIGHTING ON YOUR SIDE A MOMENT AGO?
wff
plok
sqich
DONE.
grrd
grrt

IT DOESN'T HURT ANY-MORE!
HOW DOES IT FEEL NOW?
rbb rbb
tap tap
sff sff
I STUDIED PHARMA-CEUTICAL SCIENCE IN SCHOOL.
THERE ISN'T A MEDICINE I CAN'T MAKE!
IT'S OKAY.
THANKS! UM... DO I NEED TO PAY YOU FOR...?
FOR REAL ?! THANKS!
I AM.
YOU'RE THE BEST!
DIDN'T YOU HEAR ME SAY "PHARMA-CEUTICAL SCIENCE" ?!
WOW! SO YOU STUDIED ARCHERY AT SCHOOL?
THAT IS, OF COURSE, IF I HAVE THE RIGHT INGREDI-ENTS...

AHHHHH!
WHOA! WHAT'S THAT?!

...BECAUSE—
I DIDN'T ASK A POKÉMON TO DO IT...

IF YOU NEEDED A BERRY, WHY DIDN'T YOU JUST ASK A POKÉMON TO GET IT FOR YOU?

?!

boink
KRAK SPLT
MUST BE... BUT I'VE NEVER SEEN THIS ONE BEFORE!
A P-P-POKÉ-MON?
SFFFSFF
SFF
KRAK KRAK
ting
!

DOLLAR! CENT! GET READY!
IT'S ATTACKING US!
bmp
BOM
krmmb!
WHOA!

SO PUT ONE OF THEM BACK IN ITS BALL ALREADY!
THEY START FIGHTING THE SECOND THEY'RE OUT OF THEIR POKÉ BALLS.
THEY'VE NEVER GOTTEN ALONG...

bam
bam
HEY! WHAT'S WRONG WITH YOU TWO?!

skffl
skffl
fp
pp

Kra
Kra
krkk!
krlikkrlik
...WITH ELECTRO-THERAPY!
IT MUST BE TRYING TO TREAT MY FOOT...
OH, I SEE ...
THE GROUND... IT'S STARTING TO FEEL ALL... TINGLY...
kerrrrrakk
IT'S PROBABLY JUST PREPARING TO BOOST THE POWER OF ITS MOVES!
THAT'S RIDICU-LOUS!
...AN ELEC-TRIC TYPE!
THAT POKÉ-MON MUST BE...

KRASHHH
ACK!

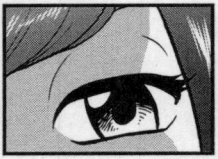

MS. ...WHAT?
JUST SIT TIGHT, MS. CUSTOMER PACKAGE.

MY JOB IS TO SAFELY DELIVER PACKAGES.
I RUN A DELIVERY SERVICE.

FSSSSSS

AND IN ORDER TO DO THAT, I'M PREPARED TO FIGHT...
...AS NECES-SARY!
THAT POKÉMON IS OBVI-OUSLY TOO POWER-FUL FOR US!
WE SHOULD MAKE A RUN FOR IT!
dash
WHAT IF IT CHASES US?!
DOLLAR! EMBER!
IT'S APPROACH-ING SO FAST THERE'S NO TIME TO COUNTER-ATTACK!
fw
sooOOh
NOW, CENT!

AND OUR FINISH-ER...
...PAY DAY!
KLANG

SIZZZI

SSSSS

ZOOOOP
MAYBE IT WAS JUST BORED AND WANTED TO PLAY ...?
YOU HAVE THE WEIRDEST THEORIES ...
HUH?
WHAT'S THIS...?

YEAH!!

HERE WE ARE!
THIS IS PROFESSOR KUKUI'S POKÉMON RESEARCH LAB.

WHAT THE HECK IS GOING ON IN THERE ...?!
HUH? OH, IT'S ALWAYS LIKE THIS.

WHOA! THAT MOVE ROCKS!
klttr
ALL RIGHT, BRING IT ON ONE MORE TIME!
tndd
YEAH, THAT'S IT!

AIEEEEE!
FWUMP
SHATTER
CAREFUL, IT'S DANGEROUS IN THERE. COME OVER HERE.
TWO OF YOU AT ONCE NOW!
COME ON!
D-DANGEROUS?! WHAT? WHY IS IT DANGEROUS?!
POPPLIO, YOUR BUBBLE WAS SUPERB!
ROWLET, EXCELLENT LEAFAGE!
ALOLA, SUN!
HEY, PROFESSOR!
OH!

AROUND THE SAME TIME...
LOOKS LIKE WE'RE ALL GATHERED TOGETHER NOW.
THE KAHUNA OF ULA'ULA ISLAND...
...NANU.
THE KAHUNA OF AKALA ISLAND...
...OLIVIA.
MOVING ON... I HAVE RECEIVED REPORTS OF...
...THE SEAFARING FOLK OF PONI ISLAND SIGHTING TAPU FINI.
HALA, WHAT ABOUT PONI ISLAND...?
THE PONI ISLAND KAHUNA POSITION IS STILL VACANT.

HOW ABOUT YOUR ISLAND?
RIGHT. WE'VE SPOTTED TAPU KOKO.
THE SAME FROM AKALA ISLAND— WITH TAPU LELE...
AND ALSO ON ULA'ULA ISLAND. PEOPLE HAVE SEEN TAPU BULU THERE.
WHAT DOES IT MEAN? WHAT DOES IT PORTEND?
WELL, ISN'T IT OBVI-OUS ...?
THE TAPU— THE GUARDIAN DEITIES OF THE ISLANDS— USUALLY REMAIN DEEP INSIDE THE RUINS.
THEY HARDLY EVER APPEAR BEFORE US. BUT THEY'VE ALL BEGUN TO SHOW THEMSELVES RECENTLY.
THE TAPU ARE ANGRY!

A Comfey Greeting
It is a tradition on Alola to greet tourists from other regions with a lei, a necklace made of flowers. But beware! That lei might turn out to be a Comfey, a Flower-type Pokémon! It's just a harmless little mischief-maker though.
Guide to Alola 2

Adventure 3
Pokémon Move Specialist Professor Kukui

PROFES-SOR!
ALOLA, SUN!
THIS IS PROFESSOR KUKUI?!
PROFESSOR?!
WHAT SOLD WELL?
OH, SUN! HAPPY DAYS! THEY SOLD REALLY WELL! I'M OUT OF STOCK!
WHY IS HE SHIRTLESS UNDER HIS LAB COAT?! AND WHY DID HE COME FLYING THROUGH THE ROOF WITH THOSE POKÉMON?! AND WHY, WHY, WHY...?
IT WAS A BIG HIT WITH THE MELE-MELE LADIES!
THE SKIN LOTION YOU MADE BY BOTTLING PYUKUMUKU MUCUS!

IT DIDN'T COST ME ANYTHING BUT TIME, SO THIS IS ALL PROFIT!
klk klk
FOR REAL?! YAY!!
HERE'S YOUR MONEY.
MY WIFE LIKED IT SO MUCH SHE BOUGHT 20 BOTTLES.
WOO
WOO
WHOA!
OH, RIGHT! SORRY!
AHEM...
PROFES-SOR, THIS IS...
YOU HAVE TO HELP HIM!
YOU IDIOT!
WHAT? I CAN'T HEAR A WORD YOU'RE SAYING.

LIKE I ALWAYS SAY, YOU HAVE TO EXPERIENCE A MOVE FOR YOURSELF TO FULLY UNDERSTAND IT!
YEAH, YEAH! I SAW IT! HOW WAS IT?!
GASP, GASP! DID YOU SEE THAT, SUN?! POPPLIO'S WATER BUBBLE?!

POP
FWIP

WHAT ARE YOU DOING ?!

OOPS!
OH, WHO'S THIS?

A DELIVERY?!
THE PACKAGE IS THIS GIRL AND...
SUN'S DELIVERY SERVICE! A DELIVERY FOR PROFESSOR KUKUI!
SHOVE

...ROTOM.
OHHH-HHH!
NICE TO MEET YOU, PROFES-SOR KUKUI.
MY NAME IS MOON. AND THIS IS...
OH, I'VE BEEN EXPECT-ING YOU!
AMAZ-ING! WON-DERFUL!
YOU DON'T SAY "NICE TO MEET YOU" HERE. THE ALOLAN GREETING GOES LIKE THIS...
ALO-O-OLA-A-A. ♪
LET GO!
IS THIS REALLY SOME-THING TO CRY OVER, PROFES-SOR?
OF COURSE IT IS, SUN!
ROTOM IS A VERY RARE POKÉMON WHO HAS NEVER BEEN SEEN BEFORE...
...IN THE ALOLA RE-GION!
ALL RIGHT, ALL RIGHT... JUST PLEASE SIGN HERE FOR THEM, OKAY?
WHERE? HERE?
Hazardous
Kukui
DELIVERY COM-PLETE!

Shff ff
pp pop

THE TAUROS RETURNS TO THE RIDE PAGER AND IS TRANSPORTED BACK TO THE FARM OR WHEREVER AND...UM... I DON'T REALLY KNOW...
HOW DOES THAT WORK ?!

THE TAUROS DISAP-PEARED TOO.
HE CHANGED BACK INTO HIS ORIGINAL CLOTHES INSTANT-LY!

SURE YOU DO! SUN, GET OUT YOUR POKÉDEX!
WHAT?! I DID MY JOB. I DON'T HAVE ANYTHING MORE TO DO WITH THIS.

OVER HERE! QUICK!
SUN! MOON!

OH! WELL DONE!

WHAT'S THIS...?
AN ILLUSTRATION OF ROTOM'S FORM CHANGES, ISN'T IT?

IN OTHER WORDS, IF IT ENTERS AN ABACUS, IT BECOMES ABACUS ROTOM! AND IF IT ENTERS A PIGGY BANK, IT BECOMES PIGGY BANK ROTOM!
NO, NO... THOSE AREN'T MA-CHINES.
FOR EXAMPLE, IF IT ENTERS A WASHING MACHINE, IT BECOMES WASH ROTOM. IF IT ENTERS A REFRIGERATOR, IT BECOMES FROST ROTOM. AND SO ON...
IT'S EVEN ABLE TO CHANGE ITS SHAPE AND INCORPORATE THE MACHINE INTO ITS BODY!
ROTOM HAS AN ELECTRIC-TYPE BODY AND LIKES TO INFILTRATE VARIOUS KINDS OF MACHINES.

...IS THE ONE I EN-TRUST-ED TO YOU, SUN.
AND THAT DEVICE, DEVELOPED BY KALOS'S FAMOUS GENIUS INVENTOR...
...BUT A CERTAIN PERSON HAS BEGUN TO RESEARCH WHETHER ROTOM CAN INFILTRATE SOMETHING ELSE...
...
THERE ARE CURRENTLY FIVE ELECTRICAL APPLIANCES THAT ROTOM IS KNOWN TO INFILTRATE AND CHANGE INTO...
EXACTLY!
SO THAT'S WHY YOU NEEDED ROTOM ...
IN OTHER WORDS... IT'S YOUR POKÉDEX!
SO I SEARCHED WORLD-WIDE FOR SOMEONE WILLING TO HELP ME, AND–
AS I SAID, THERE HAVEN'T BEEN ANY SIGHT-INGS OF ROTOM IN THE ALOLA REGION.
NO.
IS THIS ROTOM YOUR POKÉMON?
MS. CUSTOMER PACKAGE CAME TO THE RESCUE!

AND IT'S THE PICTURE OF HEALTH NOW...?
YOU'VE BEEN TAKING CARE OF IT ALL THIS TIME?
I WAS CHOSEN TO DELIVER IT BECAUSE I'M A PHARMACIST.
THERE WAS A POSSIBILITY THAT IT WOULDN'T SURVIVE THE TRIP...
WHEN I HEARD ABOUT YOUR REQUEST, THIS ROTOM WAS SICK.
OF COURSE!
YESSIR!
SUN, PLACE THE POKÉDEX HERE.
LET'S BEGIN THEN!
WON-DERFUL!
klap klap

GO AHEAD! POS-SESS IT!
OKAY, ROTOM!

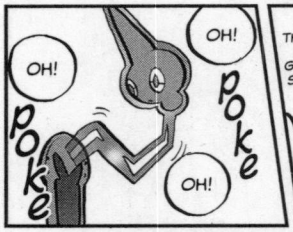
OH!
OH!
OH!
poke
poke

THAT'S A GOOD SIGN!
IT SEEMS INTER-ESTED IN IT...

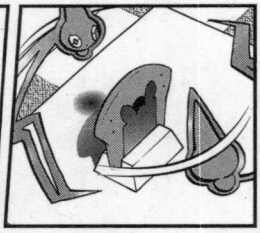

WHAT'S NOT TO LIKE ABOUT THE POKÉ-DEX ?!
HOW COME?! WHY?!
WHAT THE ...?!
dessssh

OH, AND THEN I DROPPED IT IN THE SEA...AND THE RIVER...WHILE DOING ODD JOBS...OH, AND I TOUCHED IT WHILE I WAS TOSSING THE PYUKUMUKU INTO THE SEA TOO.
OH. MAYBE THAT'S 'CAUSE I DROPPED IT ON A PILE OF MUDSDALE DUNG THE OTHER DAY.
HRM ?
IT'S STICKY AND SCRATCHED UP. AND A BIT STINKY TOO...

UM... SHOULD WE LEAVE?
DOUBLE KICK!
pap
pap
WHAT WAS THAT FOR?! DYNAMIC PUNCH!
FLYING PRESS!
SLAMM

OKAY!

GET READY!

BOM
LET'S BEGIN!
YOU NEVER HOLD BACK, DO YOU?
YOU'RE CHARGING ME ALREADY ?!
I'LL START MY ATTACK AFTER NASTY PLOT.
rm m m rm m m m
kaank
LYCANROC, ROCK CLIMB!

BOM

DARK PULSE!
SMAK

IT'S CALLED *STRATEGY*. SOMETHING YOU NEED FOR BOTH POKÉMON BATTLES AND ROMANTIC RELATIONSHIPS. BUT I GUESS YOU CAN'T HANDLE EITHER OF THOSE!
HEH HEH HEH.

YOU'RE SO UNPRE-DICT-ABLE!
ATTACK-ING *AFTER* RAISING YOUR SPECIAL ATTACK?

shff
grrr
hfff
THERE'S NO NEED FOR–
OLIVIA, YOU'RE GOING ALL OUT?!
I'm scared!
SOME GUYS LIKE THAT.
HEY! YOU'RE SCARY! SOMETIMES IT'S BETTER TO PLAY HARD TO GET, YOU KNOW.
CONTI-NENTAL CRUSH!
BLACK HOLE ECLIPSE!
TUNG
FMM
BL

AHHHH!
thud
HALA!
OH MY!
FWUMP
Ch
I'M SORRY! I'M SORRY!
NO WORRIES. YOU FOUGHT WITH EVERYTHING YOU HAD...
...BUT THIS RING DIDN'T BUDGE ONE BIT.
IT'S NOT A RING.
IT'S A BATTLE STAGE.
IT IS...?
WELL, EITHER WAY, IT'S PRETTY WELL CONSTRUCTED FOR SOMETHING YOU THREW TOGETHER SO QUICKLY. IT'S SO TOUGH EVEN OLIVIA ISN'T ABLE TO DESTROY IT.
NYYUUURGH!

...SO WE CAN INTRODUCE IT TO EVERYONE AT THE FESTIVAL TOMORROW.
WELL THEN, THIS BATTLE STAGE HAS BEEN TESTED AND DETERMINED TO BE SAFE BY YOU...

...TO-MOR-ROW...
...AS YOU KNOW...
AND...

...AS THEY DO BATTLE!
...THE YOUNG TRAINERS OF ALOLA...
...IT WILL BE GRACED BY...

...AND JOURNEY TO ALL FOUR ISLANDS TO SOOTHE THE ANGER OF THE FOUR TAPU.
AND THE MOST SKILLFUL TRAINER WILL REPRESENT US...

IN OTHER WORDS, EACH OF US HAVE ONCE FOUGHT THE TAPU.
...ALL HAVE A Z-RING.
WE, THE ISLAND KAHUNAS, AND THE TRIAL CAPTAINS...

IN THE ALOLAN TRADITION OF THE ISLAND CHALLENGE, EH?

...AS LONG AS THE TAPU ARE CALM AND CONTENTED.
THE PEOPLE OF THE ISLANDS CAN ONLY LIVE IN PEACE...

...SO I THINK THIS IS AN APPRO-PRIATE PLAN.
THE POKÉMON BATTLES HELD AT THE ANCIENT FESTIVALS WERE ORIGINALLY IN HONOR OF THE TAPU...
THE TAPU AREN'T INTERESTED IN TRAINERS THEY'VE ALREADY TANGLED WITH.

WHAT DO YOU MEAN, NANU ...?
ARE YOU SURE ABOUT THIS THOUGH...?

WE MUST CALM THE TAPU DIRECTLY !
AND NOWADAYS THE ISLANDERS THEMSELVES ARE GETTING ANXIOUS— WHAT WITH THE TAPU APPEARING BEFORE US LATELY AND DISPLAYING THEIR POWER.

I'LL HAVE ALL THE ALOLANS WHO LIVE IN OTHER REGIONS RETURN HOME TO HELP US.
THE PROBLEMS OF ALOLA MUST BE DEALT WITH BY THE PEOPLE OF ALOLA.
THAT'S WHY I HAVE CALLED ON KAHILI AS WELL.

WELL, WE DON'T YET KNOW WHY THE TAPU HAVE BECOME RESTLESS...

THAT'S TRUE...
WE HAVE TO FIND A WAY TO FIGURE THAT OUT AS WELL.
WE MUST LEARN THE SOURCE OF THEIR DIS-CONTENT.

rsty

BUT I GOT ROTOM TO COME BACK, DIDN'T I?

IT SPRANG AWAY WHENEVER I TRIED TO CATCH IT, SO I KEPT FALLING OFF CLIFFS AND TREES! HEH HEH...
YOU'RE A MESS.

PHEW, I'M BEAT.
HE GOT SO MAD AT ME!
NO SUR-PRISE THERE ...

NOPE.
SO HAS ROTOM INFILTRATED THE POKÉDEX THEN?

I'LL APPLY SOME OF MY SALVE TO YOUR INJURIES.
FOR FREE?
OF COURSE.
THEN PLEASE ... GO AHEAD!

THE POKÉDEX STILL SMELLS BAD. THE PROFESSOR IS TAKING IT APART TO CLEAN IT.
Wow! The pain's gone!
I FEEL SORRY FOR HIM...

I CAN GIVE YOU A LIFT TO A HOTEL OR THE HARBOR IF YOU WANT.
AND FOR CHEAP TOO!
klak klak

WHOA!
flap flap

SO WHAT ARE YOU GONNA DO NOW, MS. CUSTOMER PACKAGE?
YOU DELIVERED ROTOM TO PROFESSOR KUKUI, SO YOUR WORK HERE IS DONE, RIGHT?
ARE YOU GOING TO GO HOME?

... WHILE YOU WERE GONE ...
WELL, YOU WENT AFTER ROTOM, AND...
I'M SORRY! I'LL GET ROTOM BACK FOR YOU!
flap
flap
HUH? THAT ROWLET SEEMS...
... STRANGELY ATTRACTED TO YOU...
POP
OH NO!
AH!
WHAT?
?
AH-CHOO!
AH-CHOO!

THAT'S PROBABLY BECAUSE THEY WERE FIGHTING DURING THE DAY.
ROWLET IS A GRASS-TYPE POKÉMON, SO I EXPECTED IT TO HAVE THE UPPER HAND FIGHTING AGAINST POPPLIO... BUT IT KEEPS LOSING.
WHAT DO YOU MEAN?
YES.
AND YOU MADE IT SOME MEDICINE...?
IT CAUGHT A COLD INSIDE THE BUBBLE.
SNEEZING?

IT GATHERS ENERGY THROUGH PHOTOSYNTHESIS DURING THE DAY AND IS AWAKE AND ACTIVE AT NIGHT.
...ROWLET IS NOCTURNAL.
PROFESSOR KUKUI TOLD ME THAT...

THERE'S SOMETHING GLOOMY ABOUT YOU.
WHY AM I NOT SURPRISED?

I PREFER NIGHTTIME TO DAYTIME.
JUST LIKE ME.

FIRE?
twist
WHAT'S BURNING?
OH DEAR! WHAT'S THE MATTER?
MY EYES! MY EYES!
twist

OH, I SEE.
THEY LIGHT BONFIRES THE NIGHT BEFORE TO CELEBRATE.
SPLISH
SPLISH
OUR FESTIVAL IS TOMORROW.
OH, THOSE ARE THE BONFIRES IN IKI TOWN.

FULL POWER? WHAT DOES THAT MEAN?
DUNNO.
YOU DON'T KNOW MUCH, DO YOU?!

IT'S CALLED THE FULL POWER FESTIVAL.

RIGHT. IT'S HUGE. A LOT OF PEOPLE COME TO IT.
THAT JERK WE MET TODAY WAS TALKING ABOUT THE FESTIVAL.
THE FESTIVAL ...

IF YOU DON'T HAVE TO GO HOME RIGHT AWAY, WHY DON'T YOU COME TOO?
ALL THAT MATTERS IS IT'S FUN!

OKAY, ONE TWO! ONE TWO!

HEAVE HO! HEAVE HO!
rttt
rttt

DID YOU CLEAN THE POKÉDEX? AND DID ROTOM INFILTRATE IT?
YOU LOOK SLEEPY.

HEY, PROFESSOR! ALOLA!
SUN!

DID YOU SEE A TAPU YESTERDAY?!
MY BAD, MY BAD! HEY, WHAT'S THAT?!
CAN'T YOU TELL I STAYED UP ALL NIGHT CLEANING IT?!
I WAS SO BUSY CHASING ROTOM I FORGOT.
WEREN'T YOU LISTENING WHEN I GAVE YOU THE POKÉDEX?! I TOLD YOU TO TELL ME RIGHT AWAY IF YOU MET A POKÉMON THE POKÉDEX DIDN'T RECOGNIZE!
OH, IS THAT WHAT THAT POKÉMON'S CALLED? YEAH, I DID.
OH, AND THERE WAS ONE MORE THING HE ASKED ME TO DO FOR HIM...
SIGH... ANYHOW, HALA ASKED US TO KEEP AN EYE OUT FOR THIS POKÉMON AND TO REPORT ANY SIGHTINGS RIGHT AWAY!
NOPE.
THIS TIME IT IS! YOU KNOW KAHUNA HALA?
IS IT REALLY THAT BIG OF A DEAL?

...CURRENTLY HAS...

...THE FULL POWER TOURNAMENT AT THE FULL POWER FESTIVAL IN HONOR OF THE TAPU...

...THESE SIX PARTICI-PANTS...!

TO BE CONTINUED...

Festival
The people of Alola hold many outdoor festivals. Singing and Pokémon battles are often a part of the festivities. The Pokémon competitions unite everyone.
Guide to Alola 3

Pokémon Sun & Moon
Volume 1
VIZ Media Edition

Story by HIDENORI KUSAKA
Art by SATOSHI YAMAMOTO

©2018 The Pokémon Company International.
©1995–2017 Nintendo / Creatures Inc. / GAME FREAK inc.
TM, ®, and character names are trademarks of Nintendo.
POCKET MONSTERS SPECIAL SUN • MOON Vol. 1
by Hidenori KUSAKA, Satoshi YAMAMOTO
© 2017 Hidenori KUSAKA, Satoshi YAMAMOTO
All rights reserved.
Original Japanese edition published by SHOGAKUKAN.
English translation rights in the United States of America, Canada, the United Kingdom, Ireland, Australia and New Zealand arranged with SHOGAKUKAN.

Original Cover Design—Hiroyuki KAWASOME (grafio)

English Adaptation—Bryant Turnage
Translation—Tetsuichiro Miyaki
Touch-Up & Lettering—Susan Daigle-Leach
Design—Alice Lewis
Editor—Annette Roman

The stories, characters and incidents mentioned in this publication are entirely fictional.

No portion of this book may be reproduced or transmitted in any form or by any means without written permission from the copyright holders.

Printed in the U.S.A.

Published by
VIZ Media, LLC
P.O. Box 77010
San Francisco, CA 94107

10 9 8 7 6 5 4 3 2 1
First printing, May 2018

Although Sun and Moon didn't plan to participate in the Full Power Festival Tournament to win the Island Challenge Amulet, both of them end up competing. But trouble arises when the leader of Team Skull, Guzma, signs up to punish Sun for defeating some of his grunts before the competition has even started...!

Will the mysterious sparkling stone help—or hinder—Sun? Or both?

VOL. 2 AVAILABLE SEPTEMBER 2018!

POKÉMON™

POCKET COMICS

STORY & ART BY SANTA HARUKAZE

BLACK & WHITE

LEGENDARY POKÉMON

X•Y

A Pokémon pocket-sized book chock-full of four-panel gags, Pokémon trivia and fun quizzes based on the characters you know and love!

©2016 Pokémon.
©1995-2016 Nintendo/Creatures Inc./GAME FREAK inc. TM, ®, and character names are trademarks of Nintendo.
POKÉMON BW (Black • White) BAKUSHO 4KOMA MANGA ZENSHU © 2011 Santa HARUKAZE/SHOGAKUKAN
BAKUSHO 4KOMA DENSETSU NO POKÉMON O SAGASE!! © 2013 Santa HARUKAZE/SHOGAKUKAN
POKÉMON X•Y BAKUSHO 4KOMA MANGA ZENSHU © 2014 Santa HARUKAZE/SHOGAKUKAN

viz media
www.viz.com

Begin your Pokémon Adventure here in the Kanto region!

Pokémon™ ADVENTURES

RED & BLUE BOX SET

Story by HIDENORI KUSAKA Art by MATO

Includes POKÉMON ADVENTURES Vols. 1-7 and a collectible poster!

All your favorite Pokémon game characters jump out of the screen into the pages of this action-packed manga!

Red doesn't just want to train Pokémon, he wants to be their friend too. Bulbasaur and Poliwhirl seem game. But independent Pikachu won't be so easy to win over!

And watch out for Team Rocket, Red... They only want to be your enemy!

Start the adventure today!

© 2009-2012 Pokémon
© 1995-2010 Nintendo/Creatures Inc./GAME FREAK inc.
TM, ®, and character names are trademarks of Nintendo.
POCKET MONSTERS SPECIAL © 1997 Hidenori KUSAKA, MATO/SHOGAKUKAN

VIZ media
www.viz.com
PERFECT SQUARE
ALL AGES
ratings.viz.com

Pokémon™
THE SERIES
XY
A NEW
MEGA
ADVENTURE!
Ash Ketchum's journey continues in
Pokémon the Series: XY
as he arrives in the Kalos region,
a land bursting with beauty, full of
new Pokémon to be discovered!
24
ACTION-PACKED
EPISODES!
Pick up Pokémon the Series: XY today!
IN STORES NATIONWIDE
visit viz.com for more information
TV Y7 FV
DVD VIDEO
©2015 Pokémon.
©1997-2014 Nintendo, Creatures, GAME FREAK, TV Tokyo, ShoPro, JR Kikaku. TM, ® Nintendo.
viz media
The Pokémon Company INTERNATIONAL

3 1994 01580 8170

SANTA ANA
PUBLIC LIBRARY
NEW HOPE

END OF THIS GRAPHIC NOVEL!

To properly enjoy this VIZ Media graphic novel, please turn it around and begin reading from right to left.

This book has been printed in the original Japanese format in order to preserve the orientation of the original artwork. Have fun with it!

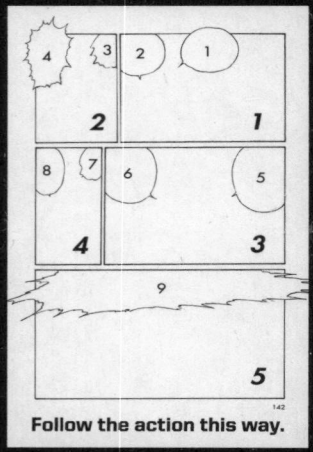

Follow the action this way.

READ THIS WAY!